This book belongs to:

....

....

spaceship school

and other stories

Written by
NICOLA BAXTER

Illustrated by
SASCHA LIPSCOMB

This is a Parragon book
This edition published in 2007

Parragon
Queen Street House
4 Queen Street
Bath BA1 1HE, UK

ISBN 978-0-7525-9497-2

Produced for Parragon by
Nicola Baxter

Designed by Amanda Hawkes
Cover designed by Gemma Hornsby
Cover illustrated by Andrew Everitt-Stewart

Printed in Italy

Contents

Spaceship School

You might think that going to school on a spaceship would be fun. I can tell you, it isn't. Imagine being stuck on board, say, a small ferry with all your teachers and your parents day in and day out for *years*. That's what it's like. There's no escape at all. After all, where are you going to go? Of course, we all have our own quarters, but how would you feel if every time you came out of your room to clean your teeth you found your maths teacher lurking in the corridor? Actually, we don't call them corridors. We call them companion ways. Anyway, I can tell you, in case you're in any doubt, that it's off-putting. It's not the greatest thing for encouraging dental hygiene.

And can you imagine the holidays? What holidays? You're in the same place with the same people. There is a room where you can go and try to pretend you're on a beach, but it's a pretty poor imitation, if you ask me. Instead of sea, there's a machine making a noise like waves. Instead of the sun, there's a huge lamp giving off solar rays. Someone with a sick sense of humour has hidden an electronic lobster somewhere behind some mock rocks. Just when you've shut your eyes and almost persuaded yourself you're lying on a beach somewhere, the wretched thing comes and nips your toe. It's not funny.

Sorry, I've wandered from the point. I've still got a sore toe from my last (and believe me, I *mean* last) time in the Beach Simulator. I was meaning to tell you about our mission and what it's like to be here.

We're on a two-hundred-and-twelve-year expedition to colonize a planet way out in another Solar System. That's right, two hundred and twelve. Okay, I know what you're asking. Of *course*, I'm not two hundred and twelve. Do I look two hundred and twelve? I'm ten. Or at least, I will be in a couple of months—or what passes for months when you're billions of light years away from your home moon.

Those of you who have your wits about you will know that there are two options here. (That's the kind of logical thinking they teach you on a spaceship.) Either our mission left less than ten years ago (all right, less than nine years and ten months ago) or I was born on board. Right second time, I'm happy to say. Why happy? Well, we're two hundred and eleven years and two hundred and sixty-four days into our flight. In less than a hundred days, we'll be there and I'll be free of this tin-can home for ever.

I can't begin to imagine what it must have been like for my great-great-great-great-great-great-great-great grandfather who was one of the people who were at the launch of our mission. He knew that he would never see the planet he was heading towards. He knew that he would have to live the rest of his life in this metal machine. You've got to admire his guts. You really have.

Later generations, of course, didn't get any choice in the matter. Like me, they were born on board and had to put up with it. In fact, it was even worse for them in a way. Not only did they only have a life in space to look forward to, but they had never lived anywhere else. On second thoughts, perhaps that was better. They say you don't miss what you've never had. Well, I've never had a planet to call home, and though I can't say I miss it, I can definitely say that I'm looking forward to setting foot on the place at last.

It's supposed to be perfect. Most of our schoolwork for the past four years has been preparing us for life on our new planet. Yes, we've done maths and stuff as well, but apart from that, all the lessons have taught us how to take care of the planet when we get there. You wouldn't think it would need anyone to take care of it. After all, it's been spinning in space for

billions of years, doing perfectly fine. And apparently, it would carry on doing that if it wasn't for us. We've been warned that our arrival will change things on the planet for ever. That's why we've got to be ever so careful about what we do. After all, two hundred and twelve years is a very long journey back if we make a mess of things there.

I suppose I ought to come clean at this point. It's not even as if going back for two hundred and twelve years is an option. Apart from the fact that this old spaceship is likely to fall apart sometime in the next year or so, the planet it came from probably isn't fit to live on any more. You see, we didn't take very good care of that one when we were there. They started having big problems about four hundred years ago. It wasn't until just over two hundred years ago that they had the technology to build this ship and send us off to find our dream planet.

As I say, it's meant to be perfect. There are huge oceans that are teeming with fish as well as lots of pretty weird creatures. There is also every kind of land you could wish for, from big, sandy deserts to areas of ice and snow that never get warm. In between, there are forests and plains, with every kind of animal

you can imagine, and a lot that you can't. Our ancestors chose it very, very carefully. It has everything we could possibly need.

Even more interesting is how they chose us. I mean, they didn't choose me, obviously, because I wasn't alive two hundred years ago. We're already clear on that, but they chose my ancestor and all the other people—six hundred of them altogether—after years of testing and questioning. I should think it was horrible. Imagine the worst test you have ever had to sit. Then imagine that if you don't pass, somewhere along the line, maybe twenty years in the future, maybe a hundred years in the future, your children are going to be the last inhabitants of a dying planet. I'm not much good at tests at the best of times. I'm pretty glad, I can tell you, that my great-great-great (and lots more greats) grandfather was a lot better than me.

His name was Epxo. I've even seen pictures of him. He had blonde hair and dark eyes. He looked sort of wise and scared at the same time. Apparently, he was good at football, whatever that is, and foreign languages. Since we all speak the same language on board, that can't have been very helpful for him. He must just have been a good all-rounder, I reckon. I decided the other day that if I ever have a son myself, I'll call him Epxo as a kind of thank you.

We're all supposed to be specializing in one subject at school, as well as learning a bit about everything on the new planet. I'm doing plants. I would have preferred animals, really, because they move about more. On the other hand, you're not very likely to be savaged by a leaf or chewed to bits by a kind of algae. At least, that's what I'm hoping.

When you look into it, there's a lot of interesting stuff to learn about plants. The ones on this planet kind of eat light. It sounds a little weird, I know, but they've got special stuff in their leaves that means they can use the light as food. I think that's pretty clever. If human beings could do that we'd never have to worry about cooking or anything ever again. We wouldn't have doughnuts, either, which would be a shame.

Anyway, studying the plants on our new planet is a pretty awesome subject. There are millions of different kinds. My main job is supposed to be stopping the rest of the crew from eating things that will

have the same basic effect as savaging or chewing to bits. I'll do my best.

Of course, as you may have guessed, the amount of information we have about the new planet is limited. All those hundreds of years ago, we sent out three probes. They landed at different points on the planet's surface and came back with wildly different information. I only know in detail about the plantlife.

One place didn't have any at all. It was cold and covered with frozen water. I hope the people setting the co-ordinates for our landing avoided that part. We're going to be pretty hungry if not. The food-generator on board this ship is likely to last about as long as the spaceship itself. Not long enough to keep me going for as long as I intend to be around.

The second place a probe set down wasn't much better. It was very hot and

only had a few rather spiny-looking plants. It seems they would be okay to eat (if you took the spines off) but we're not talking about fantastic feasts of fun here.

The third probe did a much better job. It landed in a kind of forest, absolutely full of plantlife of every kind—and a lot of rather worrying life of a more active kind.

I've made a deal with my friend Eve, who's working on creepy-crawlies, that I'll find her some really delicious food if she'll keep anything with more than four legs or less than two well away from me. It's not exactly that I don't like them, but I find it hard to assess a plant's ... er ... nutritional properties properly when something is crawling about inside my spacesuit. One of the really great things about being on board this ship (and, believe me, there aren't many) is that there are no squiggly things of any kind, unless you count the excuse for spaghetti that the food-generator pumps out.

Actually, it's not strictly true to say that there are no creepy-crawlies at all on the spaceship. What I should have said is that there are none that are free to roam around. At the very back of the school laboratory, there is a little cabinet in which a few flies are bred. They have a brief life, I'm afraid, used as food for the handful of plants we brought with us from our home planet hundreds of years ago. They're not the same plants, of course, any more than we are the same people who set off. They're the descendants of the original plants. Like all the plants on our home planet, they're carnivorous. That's why we need the flies. Apparently there are no plants like that where we're going. At some point, we'll have to decide if we can introduce our plants to the new planet. You have to be careful you see. What if our plants took over?

One of the things I'm really looking forward to is the naming. I know we'll have other stuff to worry about when we land, but after a few months, when we know what we're doing and have settled in a bit, we can start naming. Obviously, I'll be doing the plants again. Everything we see will need a name, well, probably two names. Just as we have nicknames and real names, I guess the plants will have their long official names and the ordinary names we call them by every day. It makes me laugh to think that I can call a tree, say, after my grandmother or some baby word I used when I couldn't talk properly, and in a few hundred years time, no one will know. I can imagine them, relaxing under an Ada Goo Goo tree.

Ada Goo Goo Tree.

Oooops! Sorry. There goes the siren. It means that in five minutes there'll be another disembarkation drill. We have to practise, you see. This time, it's not women and children first. You need skilled people to take that first peep outside. Then they have to advise us about things like weather conditions and what we need to wear. Of course, if we've landed in the middle of an active volcano or something, we may not need to know. I'm hoping for a nice, flat plain, grazed by animals that are a little bit (but not too much) frightened by a spaceship arriving out of the blue. I mean, I'd like them to run a short distance away so that they don't try to attack us as soon as we put our heads out of the door. Then, a couple of hours later, when we're starting to feel hungry, it would be good if some of them were starting to feel friendlier. I know that sounds a bit brutal. I couldn't myself do the stuff necessary to make a pig into a pie, so maybe it's just as well my job's in plants after all.

Hmmm, so I guess there *are* some good things about this old ship. The food-generator creates some pretty dreadful meals, but it doesn't have to kill anything to do it. And we're safe in here. No wild animals (unless you count the teachers), no volcanoes, no earthquakes, no violent storms, no tornadoes, no hurricanes. But then, think of all the things we don't have. No trees, no flowers, no blue sky. I'm looking forward to our arrival.

I've got to go now. Practice and then school coming up. Wish me luck for our landing. Oh, I didn't tell you where we're going. It's a little planet out towards the edge of the galaxy. It's called Earth.

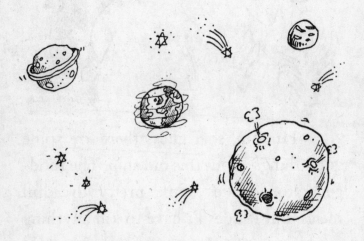

The
Alien
Headmaster

Elaine frowned. She looked around at her friends sitting on the grass in front of the school.

"Yes, but I don't see how we can know. Not for sure," she said.

The others looked thoughtful. They were talking about the headmaster, Mr. Bleaks. For some time, his strangeness had been a subject of conversation at school. "Doing a Bleaks" had entered the language as a way of describing any behaviour that was a bit weird.

Of course, all headteachers are a bit odd in some way. It goes with the job somehow. But Mr. Bleaks was much odder than any other headteacher that the children had known. He was much, much odder, for example, than their previous head, Mrs. Glood. She wore strange, striped tights and rode a bike that looked like it was made in the Middle Ages, but she wasn't as deeply, strangely, weirdly odd as Mr. Bleaks.

The headmaster had, for example, been heard to mutter to himself in a foreign language. There were children at the school who spoke lots of different languages at home, but not one of them recognized this one. He had been seen to eat *with pleasure* the semolina served up in the school cafeteria. At a recent important school hockey match, he had been heard to shout, "Come on, the Blues!" although one team was wearing yellow and the home team was in red.

There were lots of other examples like this. Even stranger was the fact that everyone liked him. It's not very usual to like your headmaster, but Mr. Bleaks took an interest in each pupil that made them feel special. He obviously cared about the school, and his decisions, unlike his everyday behaviour, seemed sensible and fair.

For weeks now, Elaine and her friends had tried to think of reasons for the headmaster's odd behaviour, but they had failed. It was just this morning that Patrick, who had been reading a space story, came up with the ultimate idea.

"Maybe," he said, "he's an alien."

What at first seemed pretty silly, on closer inspection explained a lot.

"You see," said Patrick, "if he was from another planet, he'd probably have been programmed to act like a headmaster, or at least, what the aliens thought a headmaster was like. So that's why he keeps getting it slightly wrong. He probably learnt about shouting "Come on, the Blues!" but they didn't explain you had to change it to match the colour of the team you were supporting.

"It would explain the semolina, too," said Sally. "All earth food probably tastes the same to aliens. He wouldn't know he wasn't supposed to like it."

"It would make sense of the funny language," said Raj excitedly. "Sometimes he must forget and start talking Alien!"

It was then that Elaine asked how they could ever find out for certain.

"What we need," she said, "is a surefire alien test. Something that will show us once and for all if he's human."

"In films, they test to see whether the alien has real feelings," said Patrick. "You know, would he cry if his mother died, that sort of thing."

"We can't go around bumping off old Bleaks's mother," protested Elaine. "What else do they try in films?"

"Well, you could peel his skin off to see if there was machinery underneath."

"Oh, yes," commented Elaine with deep sarcasm, "I can just see it. 'Excuse me, Mr. Bleaks, do you mind if I just peel your skin back to see if your cogs are whirring? It won't take a moment.'"

"You're right," said Raj seriously. "I think it's really important that he doesn't suspect that we know. He's been very nice so far, but who knows what he might do if his cover is blown."

"That's a good point, *if* he's an alien, but we don't actually *know* do we?" said Elaine reasonably. "I still think we need to come up with some tests. An alien planet can't have taught him everything he needs to know about Earth. If we could ask him some really detailed questions about *little*

things, we might find out, you know, if he grew up here."

"In the meantime," Sally suggested, "we should just start making a list of all the odd things we notice. You never know, there might be a kind of pattern."

Over the next few days, the friends began their fact-finding mission. Sally asked her mother about which children's television programmes were popular when she was young. She thought her mum might be about the same age as Mr. Bleaks.

"It's for a history project," Sally explained, when her mother asked why she wanted to know.

"Sally," said her mother, "one day you'll understand that no mother wants to feel as though she's already history when she's not yet forty. Go and ask your dad. I bet he watched a lot more TV than I did."

For the next week, whenever she met Mr. Bleaks, Sally dropped one of her prepared questions into the conversation. She tried to be casual about it, but it's hard to be casual about general knowledge questions on twenty-five-year-old TV programmes.

"My mum was telling me about *The Adventure of the Blue Hand*," she said, "but she couldn't remember the name of the little boy with the parrot. I expect you remember, Mr. Bleaks."

"No, I don't," said the headteacher.

The next day, Sally tried again. "How many dogs were there in *Bonzo's Band*?" she asked. "I bet you loved that show, Mr. Bleaks."

"Nope, I never saw it," said Mr. Bleaks. He looked a bit embarrassed.

Sally was careful to note down his reactions as well as his answers. In fact, she didn't get any answers. Finally, on the Friday, when Sally asked Mr. Bleaks about the catchphrase that Elmo the Pirate Cat always shouted as he went into battle, Mr. Bleaks clenched his teeth and stopped her in her tracks.

"Sally," he said, "every day this week you have asked me something about some obscure children's TV programme from twenty-odd years ago. I don't know

the answers to any of your questions because when I grew up we didn't have a TV. Why don't you ask one of the other teachers instead?"

After school that day, the friends gathered as usual in front of the gates to swap information.

"Of course, that's what he would say," said Elaine, when Sally had told her story, "if he was an alien. He couldn't possibly know the answer to all those questions, but it took him until Friday to think of a good excuse. I mean, *everyone* has a TV nowadays, don't they?"

"It wasn't nowadays, though, was it?" said Raj fairly. "It's ages ago that Mr. Bleaks was young. Maybe there weren't many TVs around then. And anyway, he might have said that because it was *true*. I don't think this proves anything either way. What have you found out, Elaine?"

Elaine was looking smug.

"I've made a list," she said, "of all the odd things he's done this week. Listen. 1. Ate those bullet-hard peas at lunch on Monday.

2. Wore odd socks, one green and one red, on Tuesday.

3. Didn't shout when James stuck chewing gum to his shoes on Wednesday.

4. (This is a good one.) Confiscated Polly's toy spaceship on Thursday and *kept it in his office*.

5. Didn't know the words to *The Wheels on the Bus* on Friday.

"Really? *Everyone* knows the words to *The Wheels on the Bus*!" cried Raj.

"Not," replied Elaine with emphasis, "if you didn't grow up on planet Earth."

There was silence while the friends digested the news.

"The evidence," said Patrick, who had moved on from space stories to his mother's collection of detective stories, "is circumstantial, but it is building up. None of these things would mean anything by themselves, but all together ... well!"

Sally frowned. "It does look bad for him," she said, "but he's such a *nice* man. Even though I was annoying him with all my questions, he didn't tell me to go away or be quiet. Mrs. Glood would have done that. And she wouldn't have been nice about it either."

The others nodded. Mr. Bleaks was a big improvement on Mrs. Glood.

"Well, we're not saying there's anything wrong with being an alien," said Raj reasonably. "It's just that it would be

good to know one way or the other. I'm not sure why, exactly."

"I am!" cried Patrick. "It would be exciting! We would be in the papers and on television and everything. We'd be famous! Everyone would want to know what it was like being taught by a real, live alien. We'd probably get rich! Newspapers would pay us for our stories."

"All right," replied Elaine. "We must make more effort to find out for certain. Has anyone got any ideas?"

There was silence. Then Raj, whose father was a doctor, said, "What about his DNA? We could get it tested."

"What's DNA?" asked Sally.

"I'm not sure," said Raj. "All I know is that everyone's is different. You can have your DNA tested to find out if you're related to someone else. Dad gets it done for people sometimes."

"I like Mr. Bleaks, but I don't want to be related to him," said Sally. "Not if he hasn't got a TV. What would there be to do if you went to stay?"

"No one's saying you have to be related to Mr. Bleaks," said Raj patiently. "In fact, if he's an alien, you definitely *can't* be related to him. That's what I thought. Aliens must have different DNA from the rest of us ... I mean, from human beings, mustn't they. If we could get it tested, then we'd know for sure."

The children looked at each other. Knowing for sure certainly seemed like a good idea.

"How would we get him to sit the exam?" asked Sally.

"It's not that sort of test," said Raj. "You have to test his blood. We just need a tiny bit of blood."

The others looked at him and shook their heads.

"Are you out of your mind?" asked Elaine. "Hello, Mr. Bleaks, I've got a knife here. Put your hand out, please."

"It is never, ever going to work," said Patrick. "And I for one don't want to start getting a reputation for sticking knives in people. You can forget it, Raj."

"He might fall over or something and bleed a bit," said Raj hopefully.

"When did you last see a teacher fall over?" asked Elaine. "They don't move fast enough to fall over."

Raj sighed. It had seemed a good idea, but they were right.

The next morning, however, he ran into school with shining eyes.

"We've got to meet behind the bike sheds at lunchtime," he hissed to Elaine and Patrick. "Tell Sally! I've got news."

The morning seemed to crawl by. But when they all met up, the news was worth waiting for.

"The thing is," said Raj, "I talked to Dad, and we don't need blood! Any part of the body would do."

"What do you suggest? An ear? Half a finger?" asked Elaine sarcastically.

"No! A fingernail or a bit of hair," said Raj. "Or even some spit, but I don't see how we can get that."

"I don't see how we can get the other bits," said Sally.

"I think the hair is the easiest." Raj had been thinking hard about this. "There are bound to be some hairs on the collar of his coat. We just have to sneak into his office and get some."

The friends considered the idea.

"It's not impossible," said Elaine. "I think I could do it tonight, when he's making sure everyone leaves the school. Give me a couple of days."

But the next morning, two things happened that changed everything. First of all, Raj came in and told them that DNA tests cost hundreds of pounds. It seemed the great idea was no good after all. The second thing was more dramatic. Mr. Bleaks called the whole school together in the gym and talked to everyone in his most serious voice.

"I expect you've seen on the news recently the terrible fighting there has been in Estavia," he said. "Many people have been made homeless and are living in tents near the border. They can't escape and they can't go back to their homes. They have no food and no money. It is up to people like us, who have so much, to help them. I'm launching an appeal today for food, clothing and medical supplies for these people. Raj, I'm coming to see your father tonight. He has promised to help. I'd like all the rest of you to go home and see what you can spare to help children just like you. Books, toys, old clothes—anything will be useful."

The headmaster paused and took a deep breath.

"Some of you may wonder why I am getting involved in this," he said. "Well, I grew up in Estavia. When I was a

boy there, we were very poor. Then a war started and we lost even the few things we had. I know what it is like to be caught up in something you can't change. We often went hungry. We ate anything we could find, even weeds from beside the road. My parents were killed in the war, but I was lucky. I was helped by people just like you in a country far away. Later, I was able to leave Estavia and go to school here. I learned to speak English, although I still forget sometimes, and have had a very happy life. But I can't stand by and see the same thing happening all over again."

There was silence for a moment. Then the hall was filled with children

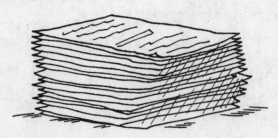

shouting, "We'll help! Don't worry!" and eagerly picking up the leaflets that the headmaster had prepared for them to take home to their parents.

Outside the gates that afternoon, the four friends felt a little silly.

"It explains the funny language," said Sally.

"It explains eating semolina and bullet-hard peas," said Raj. "Even those must taste better than weeds."

"And it explains not having a TV," admitted Elaine.

"What it doesn't explain," said Patrick thoughtfully, "is 'Come on, the Blues!' and the odd socks."

"Did you say odd socks?" asked a friendly voice. "Have I done it again?"

The headmaster had come up behind them as they were speaking. He looked down at his feet with an embarrassed smile and sighed.

"I'm colour blind, you see," he said. "I've never been any different, so I don't mind. But I do make mistakes sometimes. Why are you laughing?"

Belinda's
Big Break

Haseldene High School liked to be seen as an exclusive school.

"Our pupils, of course, are of the highest standard," the headmistress, Mrs. Ridgemont, used to say. She looked down on the pupils at Hillside High, the other school in town.

As a matter of fact, the only things that were higher at Haseldene High were the bank balances of its pupils' parents. The school charged enormous fees for educating their children. On top of these, the uniforms, consisting of a vast range of items to fit its wearers for everything from skiing to Scottish dancing, could only be bought at the most expensive shop in town, and there were always "extras" on the termly bills.

"You will want Jennifer to have ballet and riding lessons, of course," Mrs. Ridgemont would say to a quailing father.

Her tone made it clear that only a parent living under a rock would deprive his child of such necessities.

Haseldene High's reputation soared with its fees. Everyone agreed that it was the *only* school in the neighbourhood worth considering.

Most of the families with pupils at the school were used to being wealthy. When they got together at dinner parties, they discussed their stocks and shares and

the mooring fees for their yachts. They would have felt very uncomfortable indeed if they had suddenly found themselves without money.

The same could not be said of the parents of Belinda Jane Gorgle. Their money came to them very suddenly one Saturday evening when the six numbers of the National Lottery matched the mixture of birthdates and ages they had chosen.

"We're rich!" cried Belinda's father, leaping on to the sagging sofa and doing desperate damage to its ancient springs as he bounced up and down.

"Yes!" cried Belinda's mother, punching the air with her fist and very nearly knocking out her bouncing husband. Mrs. Gorgle was a champion lady wrestler. She was not a woman to tangle with if you and she were after the same single box of cereal in the supermarket.

The twins, Michael and Kent, began throwing their popcorn in the air by way of celebration, much to the delight of the family dog, a large and shaggy hound called Harris.

Only Belinda sat quietly, a blissful grin on her face. "I knew it!" she said softly. "I knew it. I knew it. I knew it!"

What Belinda knew, or thought she knew, was that she was destined to be famous. Ever since she was a tiny tot, wobbling on fat little legs as she pretended to be a ballerina, she had longed to be in the spotlight. Her brothers had been forced to sit through endless "shows", written by, produced by, designed by, choreographed by and starring ... Belinda Jane Gorgle. Belinda lived to perform. She had seen early on how much fun it was when the crowds applauded Gorgeous Grappling Gertie Gorgle (otherwise

known as her mum). Although Belinda
herself aspired to a slightly more refined
style of performance, she appreciated her
mother's showmanship and skill. She
appreciated her sparkly costumes even
more and demanded endless sequin-
sewing on her own clothes from the age of
three-and-a-half.

Now at last, as news of the lottery win began to sink in, Belinda could see that her chance for stardom was just around the corner. Surely, with the millions now at their disposal, her parents would be prepared to put her on the stage of the local theatre. They could probably afford to *buy* the theatre. Week after week, Belinda could imagine her name in lights in the centre of town. Stardom, television, even Hollywood could not be far behind.

But Belinda was about to be badly disappointed. Mr. and Mrs. Gorgle, who had spent their lives enjoying themselves without a thought for tomorrow, who wouldn't know what a savings account was if it walked up and said hello, whose idea of being responsible was to make sure that Michael and Kent went to school at least once a week, suddenly turned into model citizens.

"It's an enormous amount of money," said Mrs. Gorgle. "We've got to be careful with it. Kent! Michael! Pick up all that popcorn. It doesn't grow on trees, you know."

At the same moment, Mr. Gorgle stopped bouncing on the sofa.

"This'll last us a few more years yet," he said. "Harris! Stop chewing that cushion! It's time everyone started taking a bit more care of our things."

Next morning, after Belinda had spent a night dreaming of stardom, she found a depressingly normal breakfast table. Her parents looked serious.

"Hurry up, Belinda," said her father. "You'll be late for school if you're not careful."

"It doesn't matter," said Belinda. "It's only maths first thing. I've never understood a word of it in any case. It won't matter if I miss another lesson."

Mr. and Mrs. Gorgle looked at each other and nodded meaningfully.

"Exactly as we were saying, Gorgeous," said Mr. Gorgle. "We need to give some serious thought to these youngsters' schooling. You need an education to be able to handle the kind of money we've got. Now, off you go, Belinda! Now!"

Later that day, Mr. and Mrs. Gorgle, after collecting their prize-winning cheque and refusing any publicity, had an almost embarrassing meeting with their bank manager. The same man who had previously avoided shaking hands with them as though he didn't know where they had been, now greeted them like long lost relatives. The Gorgles were plied with coffee, pastries, an invitation to lunch at the town's most exclusive restaurant, and more good advice than anyone could

reasonably stand. The bank manager even had papers ready for them to sign.

But Mrs. Gorgle was as firm as her famous strangle hold.

"Thank you," she said, "but we need to think very carefully before we commit ourselves to anything. And now, if you'll excuse us, we have another appointment."

It was an appointment with none other than Mrs. Ridgemont, headmistress of Haseldene High. When she saw the Gorgles approaching, she squared her shoulders and prepared to deflect them forcefully from the idea that there was any place at all for their children at her school. Unaware that she was speaking to the richest couple in the entire county, she ran through the costs of an education at her establishment and skated less rapidly over the full facts than usual.

"That's fine," said Mr. Gorgle. "We expect to pay for quality."

"Nevertheless," said the head, "I'm afraid that our school is absolutely full. Demand, you see, is so great. We can really pick and choose our pupils. I'm afraid I don't have another vacancy until … hmmm … let's see … September 2015."

Gorgeous Grappling Gertie Gorgle stood up and flexed her muscles.

"I don't see how that's possible," she said, "but only the best is good enough for our children. Would a donation help?"

The headmistress retreated into the depths of her chair. It looked as if Mrs. Gorgle was about to donate her fist to Mrs. Ridgemont's chin.

"I'm afraid you don't understand," she said. "A few pounds is not going to make any difference. A full school is a full school. My hands are tied."

"We're not talking about a few pounds," said Mr. Gorgle, rising to stand beside his wife. "I thought perhaps a new science block, a sports stadium or a state-of-the art computer centre."

"But that would cost millions," Mrs. Ridgemont laughed condescendingly. "I'm afraid you don't have that kind of money. Ha, ha, ha … ha … have you?"

Mr. Gorgle handed over the bank manager's card and suggested she contact him. Ten seconds on the phone resulted in a huge change in Mrs. Ridgemont. It also

resulted in coffee and yet more pastries. And another invitation to lunch. School places for the three Gorgle children no longer seemed to be a problem.

That evening, the Gorgle parents told their children what they had arranged.

"We've got to prepare you for a life of leisure," said Mrs. Gorgle. "You need proper schooling for that. It takes brains to work out which knife to use in those fancy restaurants. Don't look like that, Belinda. You're going and that's that."

The following Monday, dressed in her posh uniform, Belinda stood sulkily on the platform while Mrs. Ridgemont introduced her to the school.

"I want you all to help Belinda to feel at home here," she said. "She is a very special pupil."

Belinda liked the sound of that but there was something else she liked much better. Mrs. Ridgemont happened to choose Belinda's first day to announce that auditions were about to be held for the end-of-term play.

"It is Shakespeare, of course," she said. "We have chosen *Hamlet*. It's an ambitious choice, but a challenge you will, I know, meet with enthusiasm. Please line up in the green corridor at lunchtime if you would like to be considered for a part."

Belinda, attempting to miss double geography in order to be first in the queue, had her first brush with Haseldene High's strict discipline. She escaped with a few stern words and some extra geography homework as it was her first day, but found to her disgust that she was almost at the back of the queue for auditions.

One by one, Haseldene's brightest and best went in and delivered a dramatic speech or soulful soliloquy. Polite applause greeted their offerings. Belinda, who had never heard of *Hamlet*, stunned the drama teacher with a spirited rendition of "I Did It My Way" and an improvised tapdance on the desk.

There was silence when she finished. Taking this for the breathless hush that she had read often follows a truly exceptional performance, Belinda launched into a show-stopping version of *The Sound of Music*, playing all the parts and skipping

madly about the room pretending to be Julie Andrews.

The drama teacher and the English teacher conferred hurriedly.

"That's enough," they said, then called, then yelled, as Belinda, hitting her stride, threatened to shatter the shelving with her top Gs.

"For which part," asked the drama teacher, when Belinda's attention had finally been caught, "would you like to be considered?"

Belinda had the grace to admit that she did not know the play very well.

"Which is the lead?" she asked.

"Well, Hamlet, of course," said the English teacher, "but…"

"That'll do," said Belinda. "When do we start rehearsing?"

"Wait! *Hamlet* is a man," cried the drama teacher. "There are only two real speaking parts for girls: the Queen and Ophelia."

"No, I'd rather be Omelette," said Belinda. "If it's a bigger part."

Later that afternoon, and not in Belinda's presence, the drama teacher and the English teacher had a tense meeting with Mrs. Ridgemont.

"Over my dead body!" cried the drama teacher.

"And mine!" echoed the English teacher.

"To be or not to be," replied Mrs. Ridgemont sweetly, "is not an option. I'm afraid that you will simply have to do your best with the material you have. The Gorgles are far too rich to risk offending them. If Belinda wants to be Hamlet, then Hamlet she will be. Besides, it's a role that a number of actresses have tackled. It will look as if we are a modern and progressive school."

The drama teacher paled. The English teacher gulped. They had heard the note of steel in their leader's voice and, like her, they had bank balances to consider.

Belinda threw herself wholeheartedly into rehearsals. The first casualty of her enthusiastic response to the script was William Shakespeare's deathless verse.

"It sounds funny," she said, "and I don't understand what it means. Can't we get him to change it?"

"William Shakespeare," the drama teacher told her, "has been dead for four hundred years."

"Then he's not going to mind if we change it, is he?" said Belinda. "And, to be honest, Omelette is a bit of a silly name. Couldn't we call him George? Or, if he's meant to be Danish, what about something foreign, like Boris or Pedro?"

The teachers duly reported to Mrs. Ridgemont that although they had just managed to hold on to the name of the play, it was now to be performed in modern English. Mrs. Ridgemont swallowed hard and agreed brightly that this was even more modern and progressive. She found

the news that the play was to be enhanced by the insertion of songs (or "numbers" as Belinda called them) harder to bear. After that, the news that Belinda looked truly dreadful in tights was less of a blow. A modern play in modern dress. What could be more appropriate?

"Belinda has insisted on providing her own costume, borrowed from her mother," said the drama teacher, blissfully unaware of the occupation of Gorgeous Gertie and the fact that not only did tights feature but sequins, sparkly bits and fringes as well.

Mrs. Ridgemont, as the opening night drew nearer and it was time for the posters to be sent out, spent several sleepless nights. The more she heard about the play, the more she felt a sense of doom hovering over her. Her school would be a laughing stock. Pupils would leave in droves. Why, oh why, had they chosen *Hamlet*?

Then, early one morning, as the dawn was breaking and a restless Mrs. Ridgemont tossed and turned once more, she realized that Belinda herself had given her the answer. If the play had another name, so that no one knew what it was *meant* to be, all would be well.

"I've been thinking about what you were saying, Belinda," she told her star the next day, having shuddered her way through another rehearsal. "*Hamlet* is quite a silly name. What would you like to call it?"

"I've always liked the name Giles," said Belinda. "It sounds classy. And we could make it happen somewhere nice and sunny. That would suit my costume better. How about Brazil?"

Mrs. Ridgemont took a deep breath and hurried off to the sixth-form art class where the posters were being designed. "Giles, Prince of Brazil" was duly printed on them.

Mrs. Ridgemont hoped for the best. As she watched the audience file in on the opening night, she tried not to notice that

Gorgeous Gertie was holding a klaxon and Mr. Gorgle had a large sign reading, "Sock it to 'em, girl!"

The performance was both worse and better than the headteacher had feared. Thinking of Shakespeare made you want to sob quietly and disappear under your seat, but viewed as a new piece of theatre the show was certainly lively, unexpected and innovative. Belinda's rendition of "No one misses Dad like I do" brought the house down and a tear to even Mrs. Ridgemont's eye. Her tap dance (with skull) in the graveyard scene brought gasps from the audience. Mrs. Ridgemont looked sideways along her row at the reporter from the local paper, who was scribbling avidly. Somewhere deep inside a tiny hope glowed that the school would be praised for its bold approach, its satire and wit, its deft use of parody and pastiche.

She was wrong, of course. The next day, the local paper led with, "Haseldene High: the end of an era" and went on to advise parents to remove their children at once. "This once fine school," the head read, "now spurns the classics in favour of so-called 'modern' art and experimental theatre. Last night's performance of *Giles, Prince of Brazil*, was laughable (in the sad bits) and sad (in the comic parts)."

So was Mrs. Ridgemont tearing her desk with her teeth and foaming at the mouth as she watched car after car sweep up the drive to collect pupils whose parents no longer felt confident of the standards at Haseldene High? No, she was quietly drinking a cup of coffee and smiling gently. She had had many dramatic encounters with parents over the years, but none, she knew, would live in her memory quite so rosily as the moment when Mr. Gorgle, beaming all over his face, had deposited in her hand a cheque for four times the amount he had promised.

"It was worth every penny to see our Belinda do so well," he said. "This is an excellent school, Mrs. Ridgemont."

And Mrs. Ridgemont, for ever so slightly different reasons, had to agree.

Music
or
Magic?

Harvey's father frowned at the piece of paper his son had brought home.

"I don't understand this," he said. "What does it mean?"

"We have to decide which subjects we want to choose for next term," Harvey explained patiently. "You can't just do any combination you like, though. You have to choose one option in each of these groups. Some subjects come up in more than one group, but you can only choose them once. Look, I've ticked the ones I'd like to do. I thought you might like to see it before I sent it back. The only group I can't decide on is the last one. What do you think?"

Geography, geology, maths, music, magic," read Mr. Baker. "Well, obviously, you should choose maths."

"No, Dad, I already chose maths in group B," said Harvey patiently. "Look! I knew you wouldn't let me drop maths. And anyway, I quite like it in a weird sort of way. That's what comes of being the son of an accountant, I suppose."

"Less of the weird, if you don't mind," grunted Mr. Baker. "Okay, what are the other options? Geography you've already chosen in group A. Geology seems a bit obscure to me. I can't see digging up bits of rock being much use to you in later life, although when I think of the garden, I'm not so sure."

"I don't really want to do geology," said Harvey. "It's taught by Miss Matthews and she really *is* weird."

"Well, that only leaves two," said his father. "Music or magic. Wait a minute, music or magic? Magic? Since when was magic a school subject?"

"There's a new teacher coming, a Mr. Izard," Harvey replied. "He's going to be teaching it, but I don't know what it means. I guess it's conjuring or something."

"Well, that settles it." Mr. Baker was firm. "Anything called 'magic' has to be a waste of time. You'll have to do music."

Harvey nodded. He knew that he had no talent of any kind in music. He didn't particularly like Mr. Alvis who taught it. But there was no way his father was going to let him do something frivolous. Harvey filled in his form and got his dad to sign at the bottom. The deed was done.

And Harvey genuinely intended to knuckle down and do his best at music. He genuinely intended that all the way to the moment when he should have set foot in the music room for the first time since he was an eleven-year-old. But as he stood outside the door and heard the wailing and screeching coming from inside, he suddenly couldn't bear the thought any more. He fled—towards the hut behind the school where the magic classes were being held.

To Harvey's surprise, he walked into an empty room. Only a tall, thin man stood at the front of the room, writing something strange-looking on the board. He turned as Harvey entered.

"I'm William Izard," he said. "You must be Harvey."

"Have I got the time wrong?" asked Harvey. "There's no one else here yet."

"No, it's going to be just you and me, I'm afraid," said Mr. Izard. "At least,

I'm not afraid because we shall be able to cover a lot more ground with just the two of us. A class of thirty rarely gets beyond chapter four of *The Spellbinder's Handbook* in a term. We shall probably finish it and start on book two.

"I thought we would be learning something like conjuring," said Harvey.

"Nonsense!" cried Mr. Izard. "You and I must agree to begin as we mean to go on, Harvey. It wasn't really you who thought it would be conjuring, was it? You just said that to your dad. You always hoped for spells, surely? They are so much more interesting than a mere exercise of sleight of hand."

Harvey nodded. He was beginning to like Mr. Izard.

"Do I need to talk?" asked Harvey. "I mean, if you can tell what I'm thinking anyway…"

"Clever boy! You're getting the hang of this already," laughed Mr. Izard. "But I think on the whole it is better if we do talk. You can fall into bad habits otherwise. Supposing we were at lunch one day, for example, and I thought 'Pass the salt!' and you did it without me saying anything. People might think it was odd."

"Would that matter?" asked Harvey, out loud this time.

"Another good question! Should magic be kept secret or shared with everyone? What do you think, Harvey?"

"I think it should be shared," said Harvey. "It's not fair if you don't pass on good ideas you find out about. It's mean somehow and cowardly."

Mr. Izard sat down and rested his chin on his hands.

"There was a time, when I was younger, when I might have agreed with you, Harvey," he said. "But I've had some bad experiences. However, it's your choice. I don't suppose your father will mind very much that you're not doing music, will he?"

"Oh." Harvey could feel his good resolutions about not hiding his magic class oozing away from him. He knew that his father certainly would *not* take it well.

"Maybe the best thing," he said, "would be if I learnt a bit first, so that when I did tell people about it, I could do something impressive. They might not laugh or be cross then."

"I think that's an excellent plan," said Mr. Izard, "now, let's start work."

Very much to Harvey's surprise, it really was magic that he learnt. It wasn't long before he was able to turn on the lights without moving from his chair. He could get dressed in a second, too, although you had to be a bit careful with that spell in case you *un*dressed yourself in a second in a public place. Apart from being impressed by the speed with which Harvey could get ready in the mornings,

Mr. Baker didn't ask him anything about how his schoolwork was going. The boy knew that it was the exam results at the end of term that would really interest his father.

As a matter of fact, Harvey's schoolwork was going really well. He found that a little magic was terribly useful for dealing quickly with homework.

His English teacher commented that Harvey's handwriting had improved, not knowing that Harvey had watched his essay being written all by itself by his pen. One way and another, Harvey had a most enjoyable term.

It was on the Friday before end-of-term exams were due to start that Mr. Izard dropped his bombshell.

"Looking forward to the exams on Monday, Harvey?" he asked casually.

"I'm not bothered, really," said his star pupil.

"Done lots of revision, have you? Good lad."

"Well, no!" Harvey looked surprised. "I thought I'd use a bit of ... you know ... magic to get me through. It works really well for my homework."

Mr. Izard suddenly looked very, very serious.

"I'm very sorry to hear that, Harvey," he said. "I had no idea. No idea at all."

"About what? What's the matter?" Harvey was beginning to feel a cold and worrying feeling in his middle. Mr. Izard's next words made the feeling even icier.

"You're not supposed to use magic for personal gain," said the teacher simply. "Surely we covered that in the first lesson?"

"I don't think so." Harvey was looking increasingly bewildered.

"Really? Well, that's a pity. Still, the fact remains. You cannot use magic to benefit yourself, and if another magician catches you doing it, he is duty bound to stop you. I'm afraid that I shall have to prevent you from using any kind of spell in your exams. *Illifillifoop!* There, it's done."

Stunned, Harvey gazed at his teacher. Suddenly, Mr. Izard didn't seem such an interesting and pleasant person. Harvey had the distinct feeling that he had been tricked.

"But you taught me yourself to turn on lights without touching the switch and get dressed in one second," he said. "Surely that's for personal gain?"

"Not if you're a doctor, rushing out to see a sick patient," said Mr. Izard. "Of course, I assumed that you would only use the spells in an emergency. I can't believe you would be so stupid as to use them for everyday life."

"But you didn't tell me not to!" Harvey protested.

"Harvey, you're not three years old," snapped Mr. Izard. "Didn't anything inside you warn you not to over-use the spells? Didn't you feel a tiny bit guilty?

After all, you did it in secret, didn't you? You didn't share these great ideas with anyone else as you planned to do."

Harvey was angry now.

"You tricked me!" he shouted. "I'm going straight to the headmaster. You can't be allowed to do this!"

But Harvey's steps slowed as he neared the headmaster's study. What was he going to say? The more he thought about it, the more Harvey felt that there were better things he could be doing with the next ten minutes—like starting to read the textbooks he hadn't bothered with that term. Only two days to do a term's work!

It was a pale and tired Harvey who sat down for the first exam on Monday morning. As he looked at the first paper, he felt a sick feeling in his stomach. He didn't know the answers to any of the questions. He didn't begin to know the answers. In fact, out of all the questions, only one of them made any sense to Harvey at all. With a heavy heart he began to write it, pen in hand in the old-fashioned way.

It was a nightmare week. Exam after exam came and went, and each one was worse than the last. In his physics exam, Harvey knew for certain that he couldn't possibly get more than 20%, as he had only answered a fifth of the questions. And of course, some of those might not even be right.

The following weekend, Harvey caught up on his sleep, but even his father noticed that something was wrong.

"You've been working too hard," he said. "Let's get away for a fishing trip now that term is over. It won't matter if your results have to wait until we get back. In any case, if you really want to know, we can phone the school secretary.

"No, no, another week won't matter," gasped Harvey. "Yes, let's go fishing."

He knew he was only putting off the evil hour by a week. All his school life, Harvey had had good results. His father loved to boast to his friends about how well his son was doing. What on earth was he going to say when the results came through this time?

Several times over the course of the following week, Harvey tried to prepare the ground for the dreadful shock in store for his father.

"Dad, about the exams," he would begin, "I wanted to say…"

But "Shhhhh! You'll disturb the fish!" was his father's reply. Or he brushed the subject aside, saying, "Time to forget about all that, Harvey. Let's just enjoy ourselves."

It's not easy to enjoy yourself when you feel that a heavy weight is about to fall on your head from a great height. In fact, it was the worst week Harvey had ever spent—including the awful one that had just gone.

The journey home was even worse. Harvey couldn't eat when they stopped at a roadside restaurant.

"Worried about your results?" asked his dad, in a moment of rare insight. "No need, son. You've always made me proud and I know it'll be the same this time. Now don't say another word. Let's push on so that we can get the suspense out of the way."

There were several envelopes on the mat behind the front door when Harvey pushed it open a couple of hours later, but he recognized the envelope with the blue school crest on it straight away.

"Mind if I look?" asked his father.

Harvey was beyond speech by this point. He mumbled something and leaned against the wall, closing his eyes. He heard his dad opening the envelope and unfolding the paper inside.

There was a long, long silence. Then Mr. Baker let out a whoop of delight.

"Top marks in everything, Harvey. Well done! These are the best results you've *ever* had! And look, I told you you'd be okay at music. You'll have to tell me what you've been doing. It's always been a bit of a mystery to me."

It wasn't the only thing that was a mystery to Harvey, but later, on his own, he opened a letter addressed in spidery handwriting that explained quite a lot.

Dear Harvey,

I felt a bit bad about misleading you in our magic lessons. It was fun at the time, but it wasn't a very nice trick to play. I hope I made it up to you by giving you a bit of a hand with your exams. There's nothing in the rules that says you can't help a fellow magician out.

It's the last time I'll be helping you, I'm afraid. I've decided that teaching isn't really for me, so I won't be there when you go back next term. You'll find no one can remember me at all and your name is down on the geology list. (I really don't think the world is ready for your musical skills yet.) You'll be a term behind, so you'll need to work hard, but I know you can do that.

I hope you learnt a lot this term, Harvey, and not just magic.

Best wishes

W. Izard

A School
for Scary
Sarah

Sarah's mother didn't tell her daughter that they were visiting a new school for Sarah until the last possible moment. She knew from experience that Sarah was very likely to go missing if she had long enough to think of somewhere to hide. If not that, then she might cover her clean dress with strawberry jam, cut chunks off her hair so that she looked like a Martian, or write rude words on her arms with indelible markers. Luckily, Sarah's spelling was so bad that teachers hardly ever understood the words, but still, it didn't make a good impression on a new school.

Sarah Stevenson had been expelled from more schools than her mother could remember. Considering she was only seven, that was quite an achievement. The reasons for Sarah's departure from these havens of learning were pretty varied.

Mugton Primary School had drawn the line when she repainted the headteacher's car. When Sarah explained that she hated blue and felt it would be improved by a coat of red enamel spray-paint, the headteacher had not been impressed.

"What really distresses me," she had told Sarah's mother, pursing her lips with a look of great seriousness, "is that she doesn't seem to think she has done anything wrong. I feel that Sarah needs more help than we can give her here. And, by the way, here is the bill for having my car resprayed. A cheque before you leave will be fine."

Puddleworth Infant School was very welcoming a week later.

"Of course we will take her," said the headmistress warmly. "I'm happy to say that our systems of discipline are much more successful than, shall we say, some *other* local schools. We believe that if we instil a sense of *self worth* in a child, she will blossom. I think you can look forward to a new Sarah in a week or so."

Sarah was at the school for ten days.

"Naturally, we like to encourage an interest in wildlife," said the headmistress from her hospital bed, "but liberating all those wild animals from the wildlife park was such a *dangerous* thing to do. Of course, receiving all those marvellous awards for protecting my pupils is very gratifying, but I would rather have the use of my legs. And I very much doubt if Year 3 will ever recover from seeing a tiger eat a

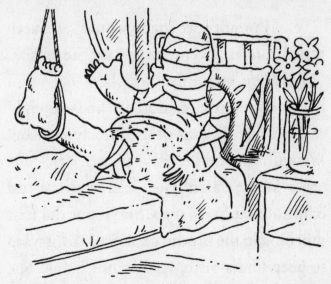

wallaby in front of their very eyes. They will all need years and *years* of counselling. No, I'm afraid we really can't allow Sarah to continue at the school. Oh, and what is she doing with that pulley? Mrs. Stevenson, could you ... *aaaaagh*!"

Luckily, the sisters at St. Mary's First School were happy to accept Sarah.

"It is teaching these more troubled children that is particularly rewarding," said Mother Joseph.

"I'm not sure that I would say Sarah was *troubled*," ventured Mrs. Stevenson. "*Troubling*, certainly, but..."

The nun interrupted. "She is a child of God like the rest of us, Mrs. Stevenson. We will be proud to educate her."

Sadly, Sarah received very little real education at St. Mary's. She spent the first morning in the broom cupboard (for trying to peep under Sister Catherine's habit). She spent the first afternoon in the sports store (for thwacking Mother Joseph on the head with a bicycle pump). Most of Tuesday was spent scrubbing the kitchen floor to remove as much as possible of the vat of tomato soup that Sarah had thought would make a good paddling pool.

By the end of the week, when Mrs. Stevenson discovered that Sarah had not taken part in a single lesson, the concerned mother marched down to the school to confront Mother Joseph and ask for an explanation (although she very much feared that she knew it already).

Sadly, this was one interview with a headmistress that did not take place. Mrs. Stevenson found Mother Joseph defending herself with a chair while Sarah, wielding a spear made from a fork tied to a ruler, attacked with all force.

"Mother Joseph says we should fight for what we believe," said Sarah, out

of breath, "and I believe in having chips every day for lunch."

When Sarah was at last restrained, Mother Joseph adjusted her veil and asked a number of questions about the family's church-going and religious life at home. Clearly, she did not find the answers at all satisfactory.

"I'm afraid, if I had realized this before, Mrs. Stevenson," she said, "I would not have accepted Sarah into the school. We do expect a certain level of, shall I say, spiritual awareness on the part of our pupils. I do have the other children to think about, you understand."

Mrs. Stevenson said a little stiffly that she understood that teaching troubled children was particularly rewarding. This was not received well by the nun.

"Please close the door as you leave," she said coolly.

The next port of call in Sarah's varied voyage of learning was Midhampton Community School. Mrs. Stevenson found herself being less than totally truthful as she described her only daughter's school career to date. She spoke vaguely about religious differences at St. Mary's.

Mr. Kirkmartin, the headteacher, smiled.

"At this school we encourage all kinds of beliefs," he said. "We are proud of our tolerant and, I think, forward-thinking approach to preparing our precious young people for life in the big, bad world."

Mrs. Stevenson viewed Mr. Martin's multi-coloured cardigan and sandals with some doubt and fell over a pile of filing on the way to the door, but she accepted a place for Sarah with enthusiasm.

Unfortunately, Mr. Kirkmartin was not as disorganized as he appeared. The next day, he telephoned Mother Joseph at St. Mary's, who passed him on to Puddleworth Infant School, which gave him the telephone number of Mugton

Primary School. After his phone calls, Mr. Kirkmartin looked thoughtful. He rifled through his filing pile and found a sheet of paper that proved quite definitively that he had no room in his school for another goldfish, never mind another pupil. He slipped a letter of regret through Mrs. Stevenson's door shortly before midnight.

It was lucky that Sarah and her mother lived in a large city. There were several more schools to try, each involving a longer bus journey than the last. Sarah lasted almost a fortnight at The Little Green School, mainly because they had the builders in and thought for a long time that the plumbing problems and missing coats were *their* fault. It was only when Sarah was caught actually stuffing an anorak into a toilet that the truth became plain. Mrs. Stevenson received her usual summons and another bill.

Not for the first time, Sarah's mother sat down with her daughter for a Serious Talk.

"I don't understand it, darling," she said. "You are such a good girl at home. At least, you're no worse than any other child I've met. Why are you *so* naughty at school? You like the other children, don't you? No one has been horrible to you?"

"No," said Sarah. "They're fine. It's just school I don't like."

"But I don't understand why," said her mother. "Is it the school dinners? I'll make you packed lunches if you like."

"No, school dinners are okay," said Sarah. "Anyway they're better for throwing than sandwiches."

Mrs. Stevenson shuddered. "You shouldn't *be* throwing them," she said. "You don't throw food about at home. Not since you were a baby, anyway. What

exactly is it that you hate so much about school? Because don't think I don't realize, Sarah Stevenson, that you are deliberately getting yourself expelled from these places. Some of them have been as good as any school could be, surely?"

Sarah looked sulky.

"I just don't like it," she said. "I don't like the way schools smell. I don't like the way they look. I don't like the way we *have* to do things. I don't like having to wait until other children have finished before I can go and play. I don't like having to wear a horrible plastic thing for painting. I don't like having to listen to stories that are silly. I don't like always having to do the same as everyone else. I just … don't … like … it. Okay?"

Mrs. Stevenson tried to marshal her thoughts. It was a pretty long list of "don't likes". As she was trying to think of what to say, Sarah asked a question.

"Did you like school, Mum? Did you like the things I don't?"

Mrs. Stevenson paused with her mouth open. For a minute she looked like a goldfish, but her thoughts were racing. At long last, she answered. She had, after all, always told her daughter to be truthful.

"No," she said, "I didn't. But sometimes there just isn't any choice, Sarah. That's one of the things you learn as you grow up."

But Sarah set her mouth in a stubborn line.

"There has to be a choice," she said. "About something important like this."

That evening, when Sarah was in bed, her mother had a visit from an old friend. They talked late into the night. The next morning, Mrs. Stevenson went to the local library and took out lots of books. She also spent a long time on the computer and the telephone. By the end of the week, she had made up her mind and contacted the local education office to put her plan into action. An appointment was made and Sarah was sent off to play with a

friend while her mother had a long meeting with several helpful people.

"Well," she was told, finally, "you know that Appleton School is willing to take Sarah, although I agree with you that the chances of her enjoying her time there are rather slim. However, if you are sure that you want to follow this path instead, then we will support you. It won't be easy but it may, as you say, be the solution."

That afternoon, Sarah's mother took her daughter to the beach. As they sat and stared at the sea, Mrs. Stevenson once again raised the subject of school.

"I've got good news, Sarah," she said, "that I think will be the answer to all your problems. In fact, I've got two pieces of good news."

Sarah looked up suspiciously.

"What's the first one?" she asked.

"Well, there is a very nice school, called Appleton School, that would like to have you as a pupil," said her mother. "It is beautiful. The school doesn't only offer the ordinary subjects. There are lots of other things you can do, like sailing and rock-climbing and diving. There's always something going on. I think you'll love it."

But Sarah was scowling. She picked up a handful of pebbles and threw them one by one towards the sea.

"I don't want to go there," she said. "It might sound as if it's different, but I think it will be like all the other places. I bet you can't go sailing just when you feel like it. It's still a *school*."

"That's true," said her mother, "but you haven't even seen Appleton. Don't you think you should go and have a look around before you make up your mind?"

"No."

"Or maybe even try it for a few days? You don't have to stay if you don't like it."

"No."

"Not even for an afternoon?"

"No."

Mrs. Stevenson threw a handful of pebbles, too.

"Then it's lucky I have another plan," she said. "And I think it's one you'll like a lot better."

Sarah looked up and spoke severely.

"If it's just another school, I'm not interested," she said. "I don't care what they teach or where it is. It'll still be a school. Forget it."

"Okay," said Mrs. Stevenson. "What if I said that you never had to go to school again? Not ever."

"Never?" Sarah could hardly believe it. "You mean, all the time until I'm grown up? I'd never have to go?"

"That's right. How would you feel about that?"

"I'd love it!" cried Sarah, jumping up and down on the sand. "No more school! Yay! That's brilliant!"

"Of course," Mrs. Stevenson was still talking, "it doesn't mean that you can stop learning. There are a lot of things you will need to know when you're grown-up, and you'll have to start learning them now. Some of them are things you would have learnt in school anyway."

"No, that's okay," said Sarah. "I like learning things. It's just school I don't like."

"Then it's a good thing that you don't have to go," said Mrs. Stevenson. "I've been doing a lot of research—that means finding out about things—and there's a programme called "Learning at home". It means that you can do all your school lessons at home and never have to go to school at all."

"That sounds okay," said Sarah. "I'll do it when I feel like it. That'll be great."

"Well, not quite. Actually, you'll do it when *I* feel like it," smiled her mother.

"You see, I'll be your teacher. It's just that you'll learn at home instead of at school, which is what you want, isn't it?"

Sarah didn't say anything. She didn't say much for the rest of the day, and when she went to bed that night, she looked very thoughtful. For a long time, she sat up in bed, eyes wide open, in her darkened room. She had serious decisions to make.

School rules were bad. But having to spend all day every day with her mother's rules? Could that really be better?

The next morning, Sarah's mother put a big pile of books on the table.

"I'll be working on your schedule for the next few days," she said, "then we'll make a start."

But Sarah shook her head.

"I'd like to go to Appleton, please," she said.

Two years later, Sarah is still at her school and very happy—at least, as happy as you can be with school rules—and she's learnt the biggest lesson she'll ever learn. Which is that even when there are choices, sometimes there's no choice at all.

Team Colours

Whether or not your school has a special uniform, it probably has a badge, or a crest, or a motto or some kind of little picture associated with the school. Maybe you have sweatshirts with the logo on. They're probably in a particular colour. And your school sports teams all wear this colour as well. That's the normal thing, but Oak Tree High wasn't exactly a normal school.

For a start, it was new. The city had expanded so much that new schools were needed. Two were built, but the other one was taken over by a smaller school that needed to expand. Oak Tree High was a brand new school, taking pupils from several other schools that were bursting at the seams. It didn't have any history at all. One minute it didn't exist. The next it was there and had fifteen hundred pupils ready to arrive in two weeks' time.

It was an incredible rush to get everything ready on time. With two days to go, the place still looked like a building site. Men in hard hats sat around eating sandwiches while the headmaster-to-be, Mr. Marsh, went purple in the face shouting at them to hurry up and *finish*. The Deputy Head, confusingly named Mrs. Principle, caused havoc by climbing a ladder to view progress and getting stuck.

Three brawny builders refused to carry her down on the grounds that they weren't insured to carry people. The foreman tried to coax her down through a loudhailer, until the headmaster, conscious that the plight of his deputy was being broadcast to most of the southern half of the city, begged him to stop. Finally, the Fire Brigade was called and successfully extricated Mrs. Principle from her perch.

None of this helped to get the building finished.

By some miracle, six hours before midnight on the day before term began, the last builder slouched off the site. Trucks had been lined up in the road

outside most of the afternoon. Now they zoomed into the drive, bringing books and chairs, desks and filing cabinets. Mr. Marsh, now pale rather than purple, tried to be in twelve places at once. Mrs. Principle, pink and perspiring, almost got run over and had a heavy box dropped on her foot. She started the term on crutches.

Mr. Marsh, feeling rather guilty, breathed a sigh of relief as Mrs. Principle was carted off to the emergency room of the local hospital to have her foot x-rayed. Things began to happen more quickly without her help.

As the daylight dimmed, another crisis struck. In all the planning, no one seemed to have thought to supply light-bulbs. Mr. Marsh sent out reinforcements to buy all the lightbulbs in every DIY store for miles around. Desperate times required desperate measures, and while it looked slightly strange to have peach-toned lighting in the boys' cloakrooms, it was better than darkness.

It was half-past three in the morning before the last empty truck rumbled on its way. Poor Mr. Marsh, too full of adrenalin now to think of sleeping, prowled around the school with a large duster and a very long list of things that still needed to be done and people that still needed to be shouted at.

It was perhaps unfortunate that the Chairman of the Governors discovered the new headmaster fast asleep in a peach-toned cloakroom at half-past seven in the morning, but there was no time for explanations. The first pupils were already piling off their buses and crowding curiously through the doors. Watching them from the vantage point of his study over the entrance, Mr. Marsh was struck for the first time by the lack of a strong identity for the school. The children swarming down the drive were dressed in a rainbow selection of garments. Mr. Marsh had no wish to insist on a full uniform, but it struck him then that the sooner a decision was made about school colours, the better. And surely, it was an easy decision to make? An establishment

called Oak Tree High School surely cried out for an oak-leaf or oak-tree emblem on a green background. Mr. Marsh sighed with satisfaction and crossed through the entry he had just made on his growing list. Another decision successfully made!

But Mr. Marsh was new to the area, and when he raised the question at the first Staff Meeting of term, heads were shaken all round.

"Can't be done, I'm afraid," said Mr. Potts, who had come from another local school. "Oakington First School already has green sweatshirts and a similar emblem. No one in a high school is going to want to wear something that five-year-olds can be seen in."

"Well, how about an acorn, then?" said Mr. Marsh brightly.

This, too, it seemed, had already been adopted by a local school. Mr. Marsh was at a loss.

"Why not ask the school itself to come up with an idea?" suggested an art teacher. "It will be an excellent project for our art and design course. And the students may have some first-class ideas."

It seemed a good plan. No one foresaw the incredible fuss that was to result from this simple suggestion.

It started innocently enough. The pupils were keen to design something themselves.

"We can go for a really *now* design," said one girl enthusiastically. Mr. Marsh viewed her multi-coloured hair and fringed jeans with a faint feeling of unease. He reassured himself with the fact that the staff would be selecting the design and anything too outlandish could be vetoed.

The first sign of trouble was when a banner appeared on the school railings one Monday morning. "Vote for Blue!" it screamed. Standing nearby, several small girls dressed entirely in various shades of blue were earnestly handing out little blue flags and trying to persuade pupils coming into the school that blue was a truly spiritual and futuristic colour.

The next morning, a minor riot broke out near the gates when a faction supporting yellow, the colour (they said) of sunshine and hope, began chanting in an aggressive manner that distressed the girls

in blue. Naturally, it wasn't long before other colours gained their own supporters.

The view from Mr. Marsh's window on the world was now very different. Each morning on the bus, students dressed in a weird assortment of clothing in single colours swarmed in colour-co-ordinated groups from the buses. The picture was completed, at the end of the week, by the emergence of the Rainbows are Real party, dressed accordingly. Their position was that choosing any single colour among the many that gave variety to the wonderful world was the act of a tyrant. Only a free expression of all the colours of the universe could truly represent the variety of people in the school.

Mr. Marsh was beginning to wish he had never raised the subject. As the end of the week and the end of the design competition drew near, he shuddered to think of the diplomatic exercise required to choose a school colour and logo.

All designs had to be submitted by three o'clock on Friday afternoon. Mrs. Principle, still not too steady on her crutches, lost her feet completely as eager

students rushed past with their cherished designs. She made her second visit to the emergency room in a month and was told that she would have to lie down for most of the rest of the term. Mr. Marsh received this news with mixed feelings. Much as he needed the support of an energetic deputy, it was becoming increasingly clear that Mrs. Principle usually caused more work than she saved.

Mr. Marsh was interrupted in his reflections by the news that a tussle had broken out in the art room. Hurrying to the spot, he found the art staff, clutching sheaves of paper, barricaded in a corner with chairs. They were defending the entries in the contest from various factions who clearly felt that too much competition was not a good thing. The battle had entered a serious stage when a young art teacher, carried away with a sense that he was defending the freedom of expression of an entire generation, launched a few paint-pot missiles into the crowd and showered the ringleaders with red and yellow splodges. This did nothing to quieten the mob. Only a deafening yell from Mr. Marsh and a threat of instant disqualification from the competition was able to do that.

We will be holding a special staff meeting tonight and considering the entries over the weekend," he announced. "This is clearly not a situation that can be prolonged. We will announce our decision at lunchtime on Monday. Now *go home*!"

That evening, the art staff pinned the entries on to three walls of the art room and the judging began. The first stage was easy—anything rude, ridiculous or otherwise outrageous could be put to one side for a start. Logos showing flying pigs, teachers with the heads of various farmyard animals, dinosaurs, a frog in a swamp (an allusion, the headmaster feared, to his own name), a jar of pickled onions, fried eggs on a purple background and a piece of writing in Chinese that, when translated, turned out to be very rude indeed, were all discarded.

The next stage was much more difficult. Mr. Marsh had decided that three designs should be selected, photocopied and taken home by the staff. Then a final vote would be taken on Monday morning.

In order to whittle down the designs more quickly, each teacher was allowed to veto up to three entries.

All of a sudden, the teachers began to take sides, just as the students had done. For a reason no one could understand, the entire geography department took against anything with stripes on it. Mr. Marsh tried to protest, but, one by one, all striped designs joined the reject pile.

The history teachers had equally strong feelings. They demanded that several colours should be avoided as they appeared to support various political parties. Huge numbers of the more colourful designs were discarded.

The art and design department, although usually operating by rules that no one else could understand, suddenly said something very sensible about the cost of reproducing multi-coloured logos on clothing and equipment. One colour, it seemed, would be much more economical.

Mr. Marsh agreed enthusiastically, and the entire output of the Rainbows are Real Party bit the dust.

By the time all the staff had used their vetoes, the art-room wall was empty.

"Oh no," groaned Mr. Marsh, "don't tell me we've got to start again."

But Mr. Potts had spotted a scruffy piece of paper that had fallen to the floor.

"No," he said, "we've got one left."

Mr. Marsh hoped desperately that it would be something appropriate.

At the top of the paper was written, "Oak Tree High School: Making Its Mark". Underneath was a muddy brown footprint.

The teachers looked at it in silence.

"It's visually strong," said the head of the art department.

"It's cheap to reproduce," said Mr. Marsh, slowly.

"Making a mark *is* what we want to do," agreed Mr. Potts.

"There's nothing like it anywhere else in the city," nodded the head.

It wasn't at all the kind of thing that anyone had imagined. But the more they thought about it, the better it seemed. There was a sense of striding forward into the future. There was a feeling of having one's feet on the ground. It wasn't bad. It wasn't bad at all.

"And," said Mr. Marsh with a look of growing delight, "there was absolutely no faction in support of mud as a colour. So we won't have any trouble when one colour is chosen over another. You know how determined those girls with the blue banners were. And the yellows and reds were just as bad."

"Someone plastered my car with purple stickers," complained another teacher, and his colleagues nodded. No one, it seemed, had shouted for mud.

On Monday morning, a small, boy in the first form was astonished to find

that he had won the contest. He was even more astonished to see the logo waved in front of the school at lunchtime. His very careful design of yellow oak leaves on a red background had been attached to the front sheet. He had unclipped it at the last moment when Mrs. Principle, hopping past heavily on her crutches and sweeping a pile of papers to the floor, had ruined the top sheet by leaving a muddy footprint on it. Somehow, it must have been put back into the pile.

The scruffy first-year thought about protesting—for perhaps half a second. And didn't.

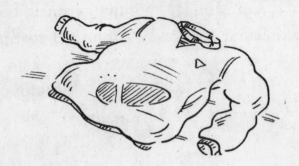